My Little Pony Friends Forever

Twilight Sparkle & Shining Armor

Written by
Rob Anderson

Art by
Amy Mebberson

Colored by
Heather Breckel

Lettered by
Neil Uyetake

ABDO Spotlight IDW

ABDOPUBLISHING.COM

Reinforced library bound edition published in 2017 by Spotlight,
a division of ABDO, PO Box 398166, Minneapolis, Minnesota 55439.
Spotlight produces high-quality reinforced library bound editions for
schools and libraries. Published by agreement with IDW.

Printed in the United States of America, North Mankato, Minnesota.
042016
092016

THIS BOOK CONTAINS
RECYCLED MATERIALS

Licensed By:

LIBRARY OF CONGRESS CATALOGING-IN-PUBLICATION DATA

Names: Anderson, Rob, 1945-, author. | Mebberson, Amy, illustrator.
Title: Twilight Sparkle & Shining Armor / writer, Rob Anderson ; art, Amy Mebberson ; colored by Heather Breckel ; letters, Neil Uyetake.
Description: Reinforced library bound edition. | Minneapolis, Minnesota : Spotlight, 2017. | Series: My little pony: friends forever
Identifiers: LCCN 2016000304 | ISBN 9781614795124
Subjects: LCSH: Graphic novels.
Classification: LCC PZ7.7.A48 Tw 2016 | DDC 741.5/973--dc23
LC record available at https://lccn.loc.gov/2016000304

Spotlight

A Division of ABDO
abdopublishing.com

WOW! A MONSTER-PEDIA! I'VE NEVER EVEN HEARD OF A TREE GOBLIN!
THE ONE LISTED ON PAGE 33?
YOU REMEMBER THE PAGE NUMBER? THAT'S IMPRESSIVE EVEN FOR YOU, TWILIGHT! DID YOU AND SHINING ARMOR USE THIS WHEN YOU PLAYED OUBLIETTES AND OGRES?
THAT'S NO GAME MANUAL, SPIKE. THAT'S AN ENCYCLOPEDIA OF REAL MONSTERS... OR AT LEAST, THEY'RE SUPPOSED TO BE REAL.
BUT WE DID MAKE A GAME OUT OF BEING "MONSTER TRACKERS" WHEN WE WERE KIDS.
MY B.B.B.F.F. WILL BE SO EXCITED TO SEE THE BOOK AGAIN!
B.B.B... OH, RIGHT, YOUR BIG BROTHER BEST FRIEND FOREVER!
EXACTLY. WITH PRINCESS CADANCE OUT OF TOWN, I'M BETTING WE'LL HAVE LOTS OF QUIET TIME TOGETHER. AND WE HAVE SO MUCH TO CATCH UP ON.
YOU TWO TAKE CARE WHILE I'M GONE. I'VE GOT TO CATCH THE TRAIN TO...

"...THE CRYSTAL EMPIRE."
I'M SURE SHINING ARMOR IS HERE SOMEWHERE.
PRINCESS TWILIGHT SPARKLE! WELCOME BACK TO THE CRYSTAL EMPIRE!
SUCH AN HONOR TO ESCORT AN ALICORN PRINCESS TO THE CASTLE!
WHEN SHINING ARMOR ASKED US TO MEET YOU—WELL, THE OTHER MEMBERS OF THE ROYAL COURT WERE GREEN WITH ENVY, TO SAY THE LEAST!
OH, SHINING ARMOR COULDN'T MAKE IT? I'M SURE HE'S VERY—
BUSY! YES, BUSY, BUSY! A PRINCE'S WORK IS NEVER DONE.
DON'T WORRY, WE HAVE SO MANY OTHER PEOPLE FOR YOU TO MEET.
YOU JUST LEAVE YOUR SOCIAL CALENDAR ENTIRELY IN OUR CAPABLE HOOVES, PRINCESS.
SOCIAL CALENDAR...?
IF ALL THE GALAS AREN'T CANCELLED, THAT IS. YOU SEE, LATELY THERE'S BEEN SOME... TROUBLE.

MY PRINCE, WE NEED A DECISION ON THE CROPS...
...I THINK WE SHOULD CONTINUE TO CONCENTRATE ON CRYSTAL BERRY PRODUCTION—
WHY, THAT'S JUST FOOLISH! WE SHOULD BE DIVERSIFYING INTO APPLES AS WELL. IN PONYVILLE, THEY—
YOU TWO ARE ALWAYS FOCUSED ON FRUIT! I'M HERE TO DISCUSS HOW OFF-KEY THE FLUGELHORNS WERE AT THE LAST—
TWYLIE, YOU'RE HERE!
I'M SO HAPPY TO SEE YOU! I'M SORRY I COULDN'T MAKE IT TO THE TRAIN STATION. THINGS HAVE BEEN A LITTLE CRAZY WITH CADANCE OUT OF TOWN.
I CAN SEE. BUT I BROUGHT SOME THINGS TO CHEER YOU UP—
I'M SORRY TO INTERRUPT, MY PRINCE, BUT WE REALLY MUST DISCUSS SOMETHING MORE SERIOUS THAN BERRIES AND FLUGELHORNS...

...NAMELY, THE STRANGE OCCURRENCES THAT CONTINUE THROUGHOUT THE CASTLE, AND ESPECIALLY IN MY LIBRARY.
OH, NOT THIS AGAIN! HERE WE GO...
LEXICON IS RIGHT! I KEEP HEARING VOICES AND MOANS IN THE HALLWAY AT NIGHT. AND THE PLUMBERS ARE HEARING THINGS, TOO.
IT'S TRUE!
WE KEEP HEARING CHAINS WHEN WE'RE WORKING IN THE LAVATORY!
AND THEN THERE'S THE MATTER OF THE GLOWING EYES I'VE SEEN IN THE LIBRARY, RIGHT BEFORE THEY VANISH INTO THIN AIR. AND ALL THE MISSING BOOKS!
I'M SO SORRY TO RAISE THIS DURING YOUR VISIT, PRINCESS CELESTIA.
UH... I'M NOT CELES—
LEX, YOU DID PROMISE TO GET YOUR EYES CHECKED AGAIN, RIGHT?
HOLD ON, BIG BROTHER. LOOK WHAT I BROUGHT!
DOESN'T THIS ALL SOUND FAMILIAR? MOANS IN THE DARK? GLOWING EYES. DRAGGING CHAINS. AND STEALING BOOKS!
IT SOUNDS JUST LIKE A CRYSTAL GHOST—ON PAGE 89!

TWILIGHT, YOU'RE SCARING THE STAFF! CRYSTAL GHOSTS AREN'T EVEN REAL. THAT'S JUST A LEGEND THAT GOES BACK TO THE DAYS OF KING SOMBRA, HUNDREDS OF MOONS AGO.
THE MOANS ARE PROBABLY SQUEAKY CASTLE DOORS. AND I BET THE "CHAINS" ARE JUST LOSE PIPES RATTLING. AND THE "MISSING BOOKS"—WELL, THE REST IS PROBABLY OVERACTIVE IMAGINATIONS.
LET'S OIL THE DOORS, CHECK THE LOOSE PIPES, AND EVERYONE RELAX, OKAY?
...ACTUALLY, SOME OF THE MONSTERS IN THE BOOK *ARE* REAL... LIKE THE HYDRA ON THE COVER...
I'M SORRY, TWYLIE. I'M GLAD YOU BROUGHT THE BOOK. IT REMINDS ME OF SOMETHING I WANT TO SHOW YOU, TOO. BUT I HAVE TO DEAL WITH SOME OF THESE OTHER MATTERS FIRST.
YOU WANT TO SETTLE IN, AND I'LL TRY TO STOP BY YOUR ROOM LATER TONIGHT?
OH, SURE... I UNDERSTAND. YOU'VE GOT A KINGDOM TO RUN!
ENOUGH WITH THE SILLY GHOST STORIES. LET'S DISCUSS SOMETHING IMPORTANT, LIKE ***FLUGELHORNS!***

IT'S GETTING PRETTY LATE. I GUESS SHINING ARMOR'S MEETINGS ARE RUNNING REALLY LONG.
HE... WASN'T SO HAPPY TO SEE... THE BOOK ANYWAY... zzzzzz
OKAY, TWYLIE. IF YOU'RE GOING TO GET YOUR CUTIE MARK AS A MONSTER TRACKER, WE HAVE TO FIND SOME REAL MONSTERS.
I'VE GOT MY NET READY, BIG BROTHER!
TODAY, WE'RE LOOKING FOR WOOD SPRITES, WHICH ARE LISTED ON...
...PAGE 63!
KEEP AN EYE OUT. THE SPRITES CAN BLEND RIGHT INTO TREES.
OF COURSE! I'VE ALMOST GOT THE BOOK MEMORIZED TOO, YOU KNOW.

WOW, THIS CAVE LOOKS HUGE.
THERE'S ALL KINDS OF MONSTERS THAT LIVE IN CAVES...
TROLLS...
GIANT SPIDERS...
QUARRAY EELS...
...NOT TO MENTION CRYSTAL GHOSTS...
I-I THINK IT'S MY TURN TO BE THE "SCOUT" TODAY...
I SHOULD GO IN FIRST, SINCE I'M OLDER...
BUT WOOD SPRITES DON'T LIVE IN CAVES...
...AND THAT'S WHAT WE'RE LOOKING FOR TODAY!

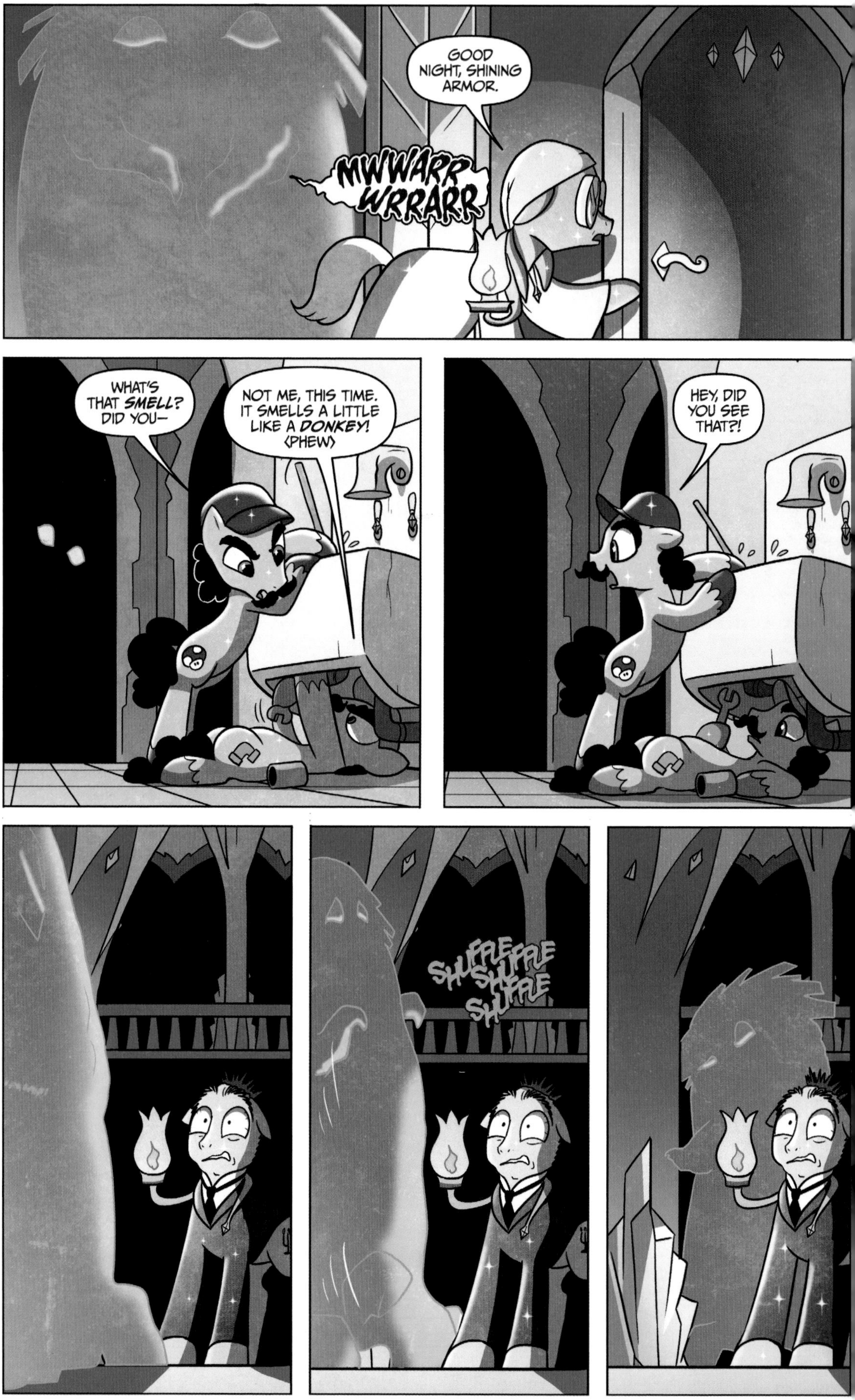
GOOD NIGHT, SHINING ARMOR.
MWWARR WRRARR
WHAT'S THAT **SMELL**? DID YOU—
NOT ME, THIS TIME. IT SMELLS A LITTLE LIKE A **DONKEY**! ‹PHEW›
HEY, DID YOU SEE THAT?!
SHUFFLE SHUFFLE SHUFFLE

(YAWN)... I MUST HAVE FALLEN ASLEEP.
HEY, WHERE'S THE MONSTER-PEDIA?
AHEM. YOUR BOOK IS MISSING?
GAH! WHAT ARE YOU ALL DOING IN HERE!
PRINCESS, I'M SORRY TO DISTURB YOUR SLEEP, BUT THINGS HAVE WORSENED, AND I'M AFRAID THE PRINCE IS STILL TOO BUSY TO LISTEN—
I THOUGHT THIS WAS ALL HORSEPUCKY, BUT I SAW IT! IT WAS HUGE!
EEP!
IT LOOKED A LITTLE LIKE A GORILLA...
AND THE CRYSTAL BERRIES ARE ALL MISSING FROM THE KITCHEN! IT'S A DISASTER!

OKAY, THIS REALLY DOES SOUND LIKE A CRYSTAL GHOST...
...IF THEY'RE REAL.
WHEN THIS GHOST STOLE THE MONSTER-PEDIA, IT MESSED WITH THE WRONG PONY!
IT'S TIME FOR THE MONSTER TRACKERS TO CATCH US A GHOST! LET'S HEAD TO THE CASTLE LIBRARY. WHO'S WITH ME?
CRYSTAL GHOSTS AREN'T IN MY JOB DESCRIPTION!
EEP!
PRINCESS, IF YOU GET KIDNAPPED, MAYBE WE'LL COME AND GET YOU LATER, OKAY?
YOU'RE NOT SCARED OF GHOSTS?
SCARED OR NOT, SOMETHING IS STEALING BOOKS...
...AND THEY'RE OVERDUE.

I CAN'T BELIEVE HOW LONG THOSE PONIES CAN TALK ABOUT TINY EWES. I HOPE TWYLIE'S STILL AWAKE.
I FEEL SO BAD ABOUT HOW I BRUSHED HER OFF. MAYBE SHE'LL FORGIVE ME WHEN SHE SEES I'VE KEPT HER OLD MONSTER TRACKER NET ALL THESE MOONS.
HEY, WHY IS EVERYONE RUNNING?!
THE GHOST! IT'S REAL! I SAW IT!
THE PRINCESS IS TRYING TO CATCH IT IN THE LIBRARY!
YOU SAW IT?... OH, NO! TWYLIE THOUGHT I WOULDN'T HELP HER!
ANY BOOK-STEALING CREATURE CAN'T STAND TO RELEASE A BOOK ONCE THEY HAVE IT, SO WE SHOULD BE ABLE TO CORNER IT.
USING ANOTHER BOOK FOR BAIT SEEMS RATHER RISKY. PERHAPS WE COULD TRY SOMETHING LESS VALUABLE, LIKE A MEMBER OF THE STAFF?
IT'S NOT EVEN ONE OF YOUR BOOKS! I'M USING THE OUBLIETTES MANUAL THAT I BROUGHT WITH—
TWANGG

IT'S TOO STRONG! IT'S PULLING ME—
NOOOO! THE BOOK!
MMMRRRAAARRWWWW
I'M HERE, TWYLIE!
KLUNCH
WHERE DID IT... ? HEY, IS THAT MY OLD NET?
YOU BET, LITTLE SIS. I'M SO SORRY THE GHOST GOT AWAY. I SHOULD HAVE BEEN HERE TO HELP.
THAT'S OKAY. I KNEW YOU WERE WORKING, BUT I STILL PROBABLY SHOULD'VE COME TO SEE YOU.
ANYWAY... DOES MY OLD NET MEAN...?
YES! THE MONSTER TRACKERS ARE TOGETHER AGAIN!

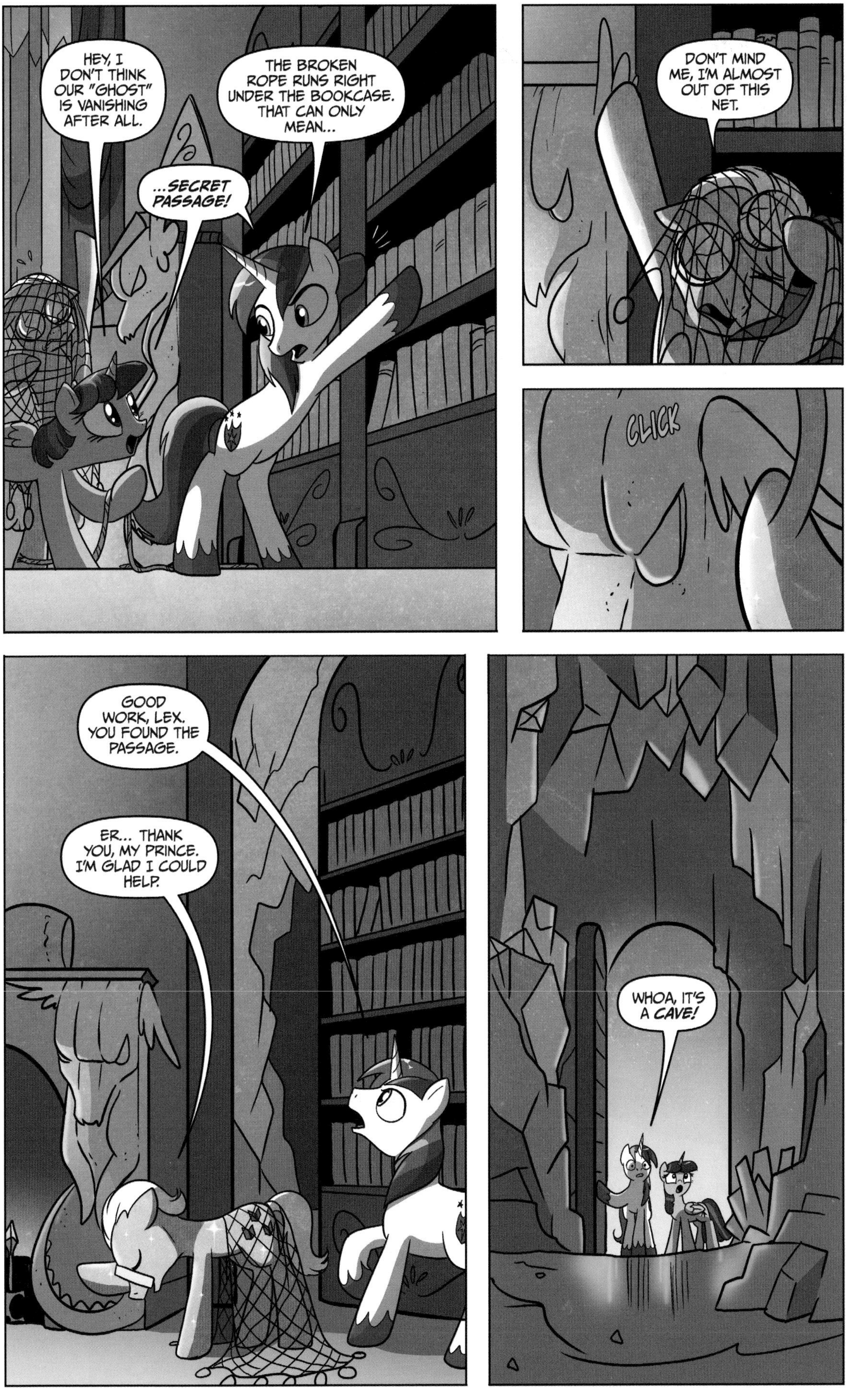
HEY, I DON'T THINK OUR "GHOST" IS VANISHING AFTER ALL.
THE BROKEN ROPE RUNS RIGHT UNDER THE BOOKCASE. THAT CAN ONLY MEAN...
...SECRET PASSAGE!
DON'T MIND ME, I'M ALMOST OUT OF THIS NET.
CLICK
GOOD WORK, LEX. YOU FOUND THE PASSAGE.
ER... THANK YOU, MY PRINCE. I'M GLAD I COULD HELP.
WHOA, IT'S A CAVE!

WELL... I'LL GO FIRST...
NO... I'M LIGHTING THE WAY. I SHOULD GO FIRST...
WHAT ARE WE? LITTLE *FOALS* AGAIN? WE CAN GO IN *TOGETHER*.
DID I TELL YOU ABOUT THE *CAVE TROLL* I SAW A WHILE BACK? WE CAN DO THIS!
STILL... IT'S VERY *DARK* DOWN HERE.
THESE STAIRS MUST HAVE BEEN PUT IN BY KING SOMBRA WHEN HE BUILT THIS CASTLE.
MWWRRRR... RRRRRR
HEAR THAT GROWLING? IT SOUNDS LIKE OUR CREATURE IS DOWN TO THE RIGHT.
WHATEVER IT IS, I DON'T THINK IT'S A *GHOST*.

WELL, MY PRINCE, IF IT'S ALL THE SAME TO YOU, I BELIEVE I'LL HEAD TO MY BEDROOM FOR SOME REST.
HMMM... I SEEM TO HAVE GOTTEN TURNED AROUND. I MUST BE HEADED DOWN TO THE KITCHEN... WILL HAVE TO GO THE BACK WAY, I SUPPOSE.
THIS IS JUST LIKE OLD TIMES... EXCEPT, YOU KNOW, WE MIGHT ACTUALLY CATCH SOMETHING.
HEY, WE SAW A WOOD SPRITE THAT ONE TIME—
OR AN OWL, MORE LIKELY.
BUT, YEAH, IT'S BEEN TOO LONG SINCE WE HAD FUN TOGETHER. I WISH WE LIVED CLOSER.
ME, TOO. IT SEEMS LIKE NOWADAYS I'M ALWAYS BUSY STUDYING OR WRITING A SCROLL REPORT...
...OR WE'RE DEALING WITH SOME CRISIS—
WAIT, BIG BROTHER. DO YOU SEE WHAT I SEE?
YES! SOME OF THOSE COBBLESTONES ARE RAISED. IT—IT LOOKS LIKE A "CAGE DROP" TRAP.
RIGHT! FROM THE MONSTER-PEDIA'S TRAP APPENDIX. IT'S HANGING UP THERE.
BUT THAT'S A MONSTER TRAP. WHY WOULD A MONSTER SET A TRAP... FOR MONSTERS? LET'S KEEP MOVING, BUT WATCH YOUR STEP.

WOW! YOU THINK THIS STONE "ARMY" BELONGED TO KING SOMBRA?
I BET THEY DID, BACK WHEN THIS WAS HIS CASTLE. HOLD ON, THOUGH. THERE'S SOMETHING ABOUT THE WAY THEY'RE TILTING THOSE LANCES.
YEP, LOOK, THEY'RE FILLED WITH GEARS. THESE THINGS WERE MADE TO SALUTE KING SOMBRA...
...AND I THINK SOMEONE TURNED IT INTO...
...ANOTHER MONSTER TRAP!
NICE CATCH! I THINK I SEE A BIGGER CAVERN AHEAD.

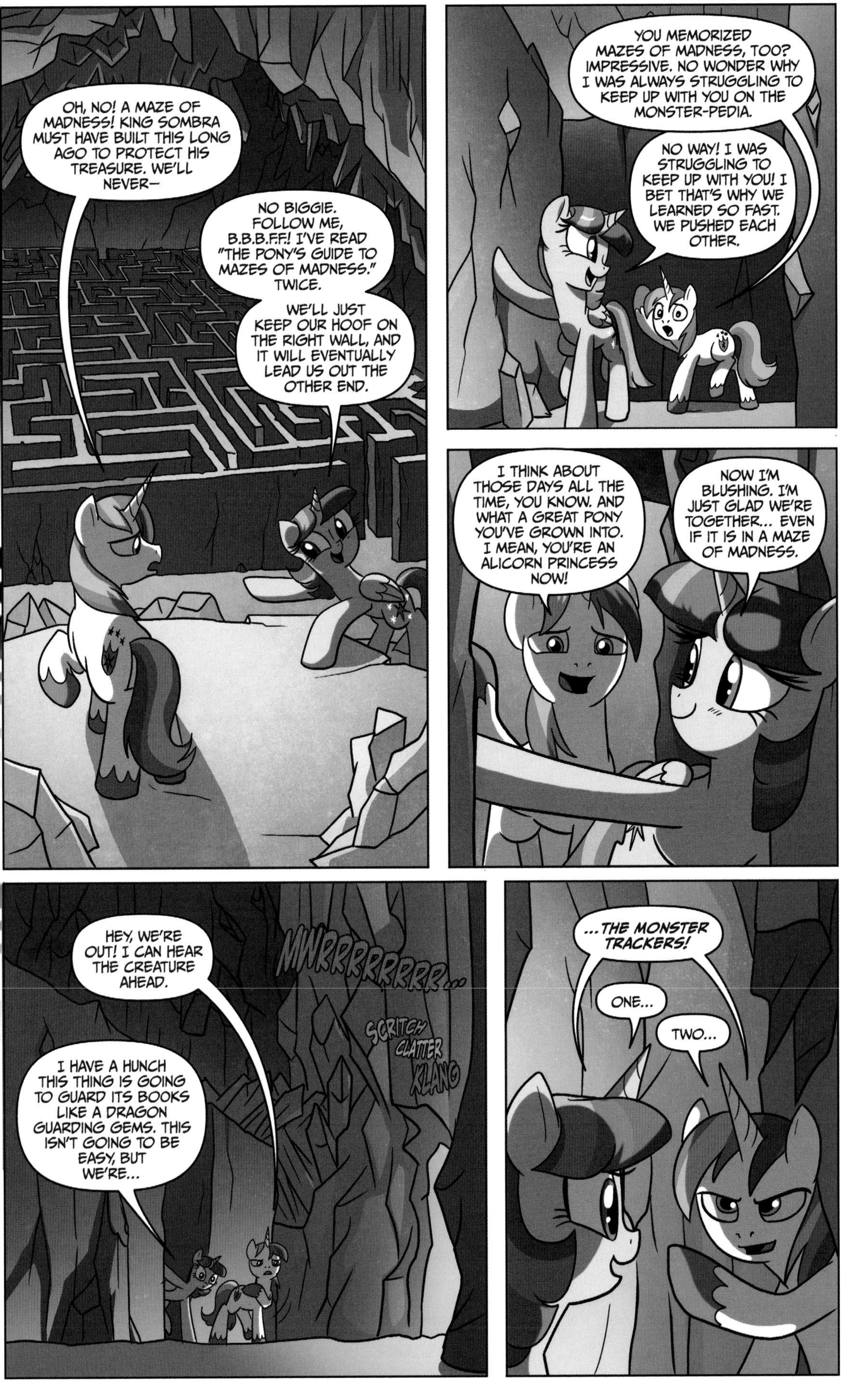
OH, NO! A MAZE OF MADNESS! KING SOMBRA MUST HAVE BUILT THIS LONG AGO TO PROTECT HIS TREASURE. WE'LL NEVER—
NO BIGGIE. FOLLOW ME, B.B.B.F.F.! I'VE READ "THE PONY'S GUIDE TO MAZES OF MADNESS." TWICE.
WE'LL JUST KEEP OUR HOOF ON THE RIGHT WALL, AND IT WILL EVENTUALLY LEAD US OUT THE OTHER END.
YOU MEMORIZED MAZES OF MADNESS, TOO? IMPRESSIVE. NO WONDER WHY I WAS ALWAYS STRUGGLING TO KEEP UP WITH YOU ON THE MONSTER-PEDIA.
NO WAY! I WAS STRUGGLING TO KEEP UP WITH YOU! I BET THAT'S WHY WE LEARNED SO FAST. WE PUSHED EACH OTHER.
I THINK ABOUT THOSE DAYS ALL THE TIME, YOU KNOW. AND WHAT A GREAT PONY YOU'VE GROWN INTO. I MEAN, YOU'RE AN ALICORN PRINCESS NOW!
NOW I'M BLUSHING. I'M JUST GLAD WE'RE TOGETHER... EVEN IF IT IS IN A MAZE OF MADNESS.
HEY, WE'RE OUT! I CAN HEAR THE CREATURE AHEAD.
MWRRRRRRRR...
SCRITCH
CLATTER
KLANG
I HAVE A HUNCH THIS THING IS GOING TO GUARD ITS BOOKS LIKE A DRAGON GUARDING GEMS. THIS ISN'T GOING TO BE EASY, BUT WE'RE...
...THE MONSTER TRACKERS!
ONE...
TWO...

THREE...?
MWRRRRRR-WAH-WAH
MWRRR-WAH-WAH-WAH-WAH

THIS IS THE CRYSTAL GHOST? I IMAGINED LESS... CRYING WHEN WE FOUND HIM.
DON'T WORRY, NO ONE'S GOING TO HURT YOU. WHAT'S WRONG, CRYSTAL... GUY?
YOU... MWRR... MADE IT THROUGH ALL THE TRAPS AND FOUND... MWRR... ME.
PLEASE DON'T TAKE... MWRR... ME BACK TO KING SOMBRA!
SOMBRA? HE'S BEEN OFF THE THRONE FOR HUNDREDS OF MOONS! AND EVEN WHEN HE RETURNED, WE DEFEATED HIM.
KING SOMBRA IS GONE?
YOU-YOU... MWRR... MEAN, I'M FREE?
WHAT DO YOU MEAN BY "FREE"?
"MWRR... MANY MOONS AGO, I WAS CAPTURED BY KING SOMBRA. HE HAD BEEN HUNTING FOR A CRYSTAL BARD, LIKE MWRR... ME.
"WE'RE SOLITARY BY NATURE, EXCEPT WHEN WE PERFORM, AND OUR VOICES ARE KNOWN TO SOOTHE EVEN THE MWRR... MOST UNPLEASANT OF CREATURES.

"HE TREATED MWRR... ME LIKE A PET, MWRR... MAKING ME READ TO HIM. LUCKILY, I LOVE TO READ OUT LOUD...
"...BUT HE WAS STILL MWRR... MEAN. AND KIND OF SMELLY.
"ONE DAY, I ACCIDENTALLY DISCOVERED THE SECRET PASSAGEWAY TO THE CAVES BELOW THE CASTLE...
"...AND WITH A PLACE TO HIDE, I SNAPPED MWRR... MY CHAIN AND RAN.
"EVEN WHEN SOMBRA SET THOSE TRAPS DOWN HERE, HE COULDN'T CATCH MWRR... ME AGAIN.
"I LEARNED TO AVOID THEM AND FOUND A WAY THROUGH THE MWRR... MAZE."
I'VE BEEN HIDING EVER SINCE.
I'M SORRY I STOLE THE BOOKS! I ALWAYS RETURNED THEM... EVENTUALLY...

AH, FINALLY! I REALLY DON'T REMEMBER THERE BEING SO MANY TURNS, GOING THE BACK WAY.
DON'T WORRY ABOUT THE BOOKS...
...I'M JUST GLAD WE FOUND YOU—THANKS TO TWYLIE.
YOU MUST HAVE BECOME A LEGEND IN EQUESTRIA DURING THE THOUSAND MOONS THE CRYSTAL EMPIRE DISAPPEARED. THOUGH YOU WERE LISTED UNDER "GHOSTS" IN OUR MONSTER-PEDIA. I'LL NEED TO SEND A CORRECTION TO THE—
BUT... IF SOMBRA IS GONE-IF I DON'T NEED TO HIDE ANYMORE, I-I DON'T EVEN KNOW WHAT I'M GOING TO DO.
WE JUST NEED TO FIND YOU A JOB!
IT DOES LOOK LIKE SOMEONE'S GOING TO NEED TO RESHELVE A *LOT* OF OVERDUE BOOKS.
!?
DID SOMEONE MENTION *OVERDUE BOOKS?*
...
AND WHAT ARE YOU ALL DOING IN MY BEDROOM?
!?

THE NEXT DAY...
I SEE SOMEONE HAS FOUND A JOB TO DO.
HE'S A WIZARD WITH THE BOOKS; HE KNOWS EVERY ONE BY HEART. PLUS, HE'S PERFORMING AT STORY-TIME TONIGHT!
MMRRR RRRWN
HERE'S THE NEXT BATCH READY FOR RESHELVING.
I WISH YOU COULD STAY LONGER.
ME, TOO. BUT WE BOTH HAVE THINGS TO DO. AND WE CAN VISIT AGAIN SOON. I'M NOT GOING TO LET DISTANCE OR "GROWN-UP" STUFF KEEP ME AWAY FROM MY B.B.B.F.F. FOR LONG.
I'M JUST SORRY MY "GROWN-UP" RESPONSIBILITIES ALMOST MADE ME FORGET WHAT'S REALLY IMPORTANT TO ME. LIKE TRACKING MONSTERS... WITH MY LITTLE SIS.
HEY, YOU FIND ANOTHER MONSTER, I'LL BE HERE IN A FLASH!
IT'S GETTING DARK. WATCH OUT FOR *NIGHT SPRITES*. YOU KNOW HOW THEY LOVE TRAINS!
YEP, THEY'RE LISTED ON...
PAGE 113!
The End.